Sarah the Spider's Christmas Surprise

Hilary Robinson · Illustration Jane Abbott

Belitha Press

Sarah the Spider could always be found
Darning her stockings when Christmas came round,
Ready for Santa, who might on his way,
Drop in with some gifts from his magical sleigh.

This year was to be no exception
As Sarah arranged her official reception.
Her friends all lined up as she danced about,
Skipping with tinsel and handing it out.

Even the mice were allowed to take part,
At Christmas time the friends were all heart,
This was the season of goodwill to all
For friends and for foes, those big and those small.

'Right,' Sarah said, 'there's no time to waste.
We've so much to do but first we must paste
The posters to show the date and the time
Of my annual event, the barn pantomime!'

'And if you don't mind I'll prepare for the show
I've got so much to do with one day to go.
I'm off to the duck pond with all of these bags,
With some of my props and bundles of rags.'

'What's Sarah up to?' asked Old Mother Hen.
'We're all in this barn because our old pen
Is frozen with ice and there's such a strong breeze
If she stays out too long she's likely to freeze!'

Barney Owl glanced up and shouted aloud,
'You'll find out tomorrow, I'm sure you'll be proud.
Now let's pull together, there are jobs to be done,
And by helping each other it's bound to be fun.'

The friends decked the barn throughout the day
With cowbells and garlands of holly and hay.
The doves and robins lined up on barrels
To sing festive songs and bright Christmas carols.

'Will Santa be hungry?' asked Larry the Lamb.
'I could ask Mother Hen for some of her jam.
If we have bread for tea I could save him mine
Together with cake and a drop of pear wine.'

'And don't forget Rudolph!' quacked Dicky the Duck,
Who'd made a new home in the back of a truck.
'The pond is iced up and there are mountains of snow
His hoofs might be numb with so far to go.'

Larry nodded his head and said, 'I think I know
What'll warm up his hoofs and make his nose glow.
A drop of hot punch, as well as a bowl
Of the best pumpkin soup with a crusty warm roll.'

Later that evening, exhausted and cold,
Sarah returned to the welcoming fold,
But there was one job she still had to do,
She sneaked from the barn with a note in her shoe.

She ran to the house where the local church choir
Were singing aloud round a lovely warm fire.
She crawled to the hearth and up on the logs
Avoiding the paws of the resting farm dogs.

Up by the chimney she re-read her note,
Kissed it and hugged it and then let it float
Away in the smoke for Santa to read
About her great show and what she would need.

In a hasty retreat she ran through the snow
Excited on this, the eve of her show.
And through the dark sky the moon shone bright,
Spotting our star with brilliant light.

The friends all looked up so pleased to see
That Sarah was back and Barney said he
Had just read a book enjoyed by them all,
Which told the tale of a girl who went to a ball.

'It's now rather late so let's all go to bed
And hang up your stockings,' he eagerly said.
The friends settled down with two thoughts in mind
Had they been good and would Santa be kind?

Tired and excited they all fell asleep,
And even the lambs and their mothers, the sheep,
Dreamed that Santa would stop in his tracks
And fill up their stockings and hessian sacks!

The barn was quiet throughout that long night
Not a whisper was heard as the friends all slept tight,
But as Christmas Day dawned and church bells rang out,
The wide awake friends were leaping about.

Paper and ribbons were strewn all around
As gifts were unwrapped, and Sarah then found
That instead of eight stockings filled to the top
She had one gift in each and a cracker to pop!

The friends crowded round eager to see
What each present was, what could it be?
In no time at all Sarah opened all eight
And found for each foot a shiny ice skate!

With a whoop and a scream she ran to the pond
With costumes in hand, her props and a wand.
The friends ran behind, including the mice,
To see her perform...Cinderella On Ice!

First published in the UK in 1999 by
Belitha Press Limited, London House, Great Eastern Wharf,
Parkgate Road, London SW11 4NQ.

ISBN 1 84138 100 4 (hardback)
ISBN 1 84138 044 X (paperback)

British Library Cataloguing in Publication Data for this
book is available from the British Library

Printed in Hong Kong

Editor: Honor Head
Designer: Simeen Karim